T0171699

THE DAY
Loneliness Is A Cruel Friend

THERESA PEERY

WESTBOW
PRESS®
A DIVISION OF THOMAS NELSON
& ZONDERVAN

WestBow Press books may be ordered through booksellers or by contacting:

WestBow Press
A Division of Thomas Nelson & Zondervan
1663 Liberty Drive
Bloomington, IN 47403
www.westbowpress.com
1 (866) 928-1240

Scripture taken from the King James Version of the Bible.

ISBN: 978-1-5127-2799-9 (sc)

Library of Congress Control Number: 2016900966

Print information available on the last page.

WestBow Press rev. date: 2/23/2016

INTRODUCTION

From the betrayal of a broken family, to the fear and hopelessness of alcoholism, to the loss of a loved one by death----how can we cope? How can we put our families, our marriages, our lives back together? How can we cope with the loss of a loved one? A child? How can we even hope to achieve deliverance from the plague of fear and hopelessness that loneliness dictates to us? Herein is hope:

"Thou wilt keep him in perfect peace, whose mind is stayed on Thee: because he trusteth in Thee."—Isaiah 26:3

"Peace I leave with you, My peace I give unto you: NOT as the world giveth give I unto you. Let NOT your heart be troubled, neither let it be afraid."---John 14:27

"But My God SHALL supply ALL your need according to His riches in glory by Christ Jesus."---Philippians 4:19

Peace be unto you, my friend!!

Theresa Peery

QUENTIN
(Too Much Is Not Enough)

It was a cool autumn morning~~
and little 7yr old Quentin wanted
so badly to have interaction with
someone~~ANYONE`! He was so bored
(in their suburban home trying to
entertain himself as best he could.)
Dad was the chief provider and
mom was always busying herself
with things around the house.

He had all the latest game systems and
games; knew how to use a computer;
and had all the art supplies he could
ever hope for. But, no matter how much
you have ~~ it gets quite lonely and
boring doing things all by yourself!
Just to have a friend he could invite
over or be invited out would mean
SO much to this little guy. But mom
was so fearful. (He'd been somewhat
cloistered all of his life because mom
was afraid of losing him. ~ She had

almost died from losing her first child;
and couldn't bear to lose him, too!)

But here was little Quentin! He knew
mom and dad loved him ~~ so why was
he so lonely? Was this the way life was
supposed to be? It just didn't seem fair!

To show his need of companionship,
he often became very antsy and acted
out ~ causing great stress for mom
and dad! What else could he do to let
them know that he just wanted to be
normal~~ like every other child he'd
ever seen!? He was such a bright little
guy, and had SO much to offer~~ but
had no one to show his abilities to.

Dad and mom had tried to give him the
best~~~they just wanted him safe!! (and
the world's NOT a safe place, as we all
know!) They had even been schooling
Quentin at home to try to keep him
from getting hurt; but, at times, this
little guy just felt like he'd always been
bad and needed to be jailed. He didn't
know how to prove to them that he'd
be okay; that he could be trusted out

3

or their sight occasionally. He didn't want to be away from them~~ just to be able to explore and do the things that normal little boys his age could do. Oh!! How he longed to be normal!!!

Well, autumn came and autumn went with no real changes. Winter came and went with no real changes, either. Quentin had just about given up ALL hope of ever being normal~ and NOT being lonely & bored anymore. Now he was downright ANGRY!! Angry at mom and dad; angry at the world~~ and most of all: angry at God!! How could God send him down here just to be bored and alone ALL THE TIME!! He couldn't be a very good God if He wanted His people to live like this all the time!!!

Quentin began to really lash out at mom and dad (thinking that they really didn't love him after all; but just provided for him because they had to, and to keep him quiet! ~~ (Which really didn't work as well as they thought it would!!) He started really becoming mean and mouthy. He'd often scream whatever came into his mind without ANY forethought of who it might hurt. (After all~~ he was hurting; so why shouldn't everyone else be hurting? ~ At least that would be fair, anyway!!)

He began destroying everything he'd ever been given. (Mom's and dad's things, too.) He started throwing tantrums like never before; that would cause holes in the walls and windows of their home. "Maybe now mom and dad will be able to hear my heart." He thought. At times he might even hit mom or dad, just to let them know that he was still there and still needed them. This did little to change things though~~other than to anger mom and dad; who said if he didn't stop they'd be forced to take action.

"What action?" thought Quentin "Putting me in jail or a home for children? Well; at least in a children's home, I'd be able to find a friend to be with!" So he continued with his newly found remedy for loneliness and anger.

Chapter 2
THE UNWELCOMED ADVICE

Finally one day when his parents were out shopping, (Quentin had stayed with relatives because they feared to take him along); mom and dad met up with an old friend they hadn't visited with for a long time—certainly since before all these problems arose with Quentin!--So they decided to visit over lunch and see what suggestions their friend could offer them for their 'Quentin problem'!

After explaining to their friend their view of the problem---they were surprised to hear the solution their friend offered: "Sounds like he needs a friend!" he told them.

"He needs a friend? What about us?" they thought. "We don't know what to do or say to get him to just 'chill-out! And he thinks we should just give in and let him do whatever he wants with someone else to help him? What about the tantrums and destruction~~the havaak he reeks? He's hurt us badly~~ ripped our hearts right out of our chests, and doesn't even say he's sorry! They're not even TRYING to help us---they're only on HIS side!! No one hears our pain!!!"

They returned home more hurt, confused, and angry than ever. "We poured our hearts out to our 'SO-CALLED' friends---and they didn't even hear us! If that's the way friends are~~~WHO NEEDS 'EM?"

After dinner was completed—and Quentin was bathed and tucked into bed—they went to bed themselves; (they had determined to take Quentin to a child psychiatrist~~they'd get him an appointment tomorrow). "He must be losing his mind! That's the only way any of this makes any sense!" They snuggled down under the blankets, determined to put the problems out their minds; (even if only for tonight); but sleep eluded them. Their minds rehashed all the events of the last few months; trying to find another answer.

Quentin had been such a sweet, loving child. Why had he turned out this way? It couldn't be their fault! They had ALWAYS tried to provide for him the best they knew how~~~given him nearly everything he'd ever wanted. This just couldn't be on them; could it?!

When the alarm went off the next morning; they were tempted to just sleep in (after all, they were so-o-o-o-o exhausted)! Then they remembered the decision they'd made last night~~the decision to seek professional psychiatric help for Quentin.

They woke Quentin up for breakfast; but he refused to eat. "I'm just NOT hungry!!" he told them; and went on into his video game. They went to him and tried to talk--- but he ignored them and continued to play with (& talk to) his video game.

Chapter 3
THE NEW FRIEND

Mom and dad left to return to the kitchen and discuss what they were going to do. They picked up the phone and dialed the number of the most highly recommended child psychiatrist in town, (Dr. Toymann). "We need someone who can find out what's wrong with our little Quentin. He's just 7; (er...almost 8)—and a little monster. He used to be such a sweet and loving little boy. We don't know how to reach him~~~ NOTHING IS WORKING!" "Okay, how about bringing him into my office around 10am on Wednesday. I'll need to speak with the two of you first-to get some preliminary information. Don't worry about Quentin~~ I have a wonderful assistant who usually knows how to get children to loosen up and relax. Quentin will be fine while we're talking; I promise!" –This was Monday, February 20.

On Wednesday, February 22; mom and dad packed little Quentin up in the car and drove about 30 minutes to the doctor's office. ~~~~"What is this place?" asked Quentin. "It's a friend mommy and daddy have to talk to for a while. Don't worry, honey, we won't be long, we promise!"

"What? ANOTHER friend for mom and dad? That wasn't fair!!! Someone else to take them away from him!! Why was he not allowed any friends---was he THAT bad?"

Dejected and depressed, he walked into the office with his parents—who were met immediately by a sharp-dressed man. *"I guess mommy and daddy don't want any friends younger than they are----especially as young as me!"* He *thought to himself. "I wish I'd never been born! Then I wouldn't have to be alone!!"* As mom and dad went into another room with their 'new friend'; Quentin sat there on a hard chair. (Oh! It was padded, and looked mighty comfortable--- but to Quentin it felt like it was made of stone); NOTHING was comfortable anymore!! Quentin was sitting there 'ALONE AGAIN'—with, big old 'alligator tears' flooding his cheeks when an older boy walked up.

"What's your name, little boy? My name is Harold~~but they call me 'Harry the Merry man!" the boy told him.

"Quentin, why? What's it matter anyway?" Quentin replied.

"I just thought you looked like you needed someone to talk to. I live here— our house is upstairs." Harry told him.

"Oh! I thought this was some kind of an office." said Quentin. "Oh! It is. My dad's office, I just come down here to try to make friends when parents bring their children in while they talk to my dad," said Harry. "Do you like to draw? I sure do! Do you want to come to the table with me? We've got pencils, crayons, markers; and lots of paper and coloring books. You wanna try it?"

"Okay; sounds great—maybe it will be fun. At least I won't have to do it by myself again THIS time!" He thought.

The two boys left the chairs and went over to the table; where Harry asked Quentin about his family. Quentin refused to talk about it~~stating: "You don't REALLY want to know~~~~it's TOO BORING to talk about!!"

They picked up paper, pencils, and crayons; and Harry proceeded to draw pictures of his family; (just he and dad- mom had passed away right after he was born) ~~~but Harry seemed to have a great life! He drew pictures of happy times with dad: fishing, playing games, watching TV together, and- just talking!) He drew pictures of happy relatives around a table of special food-~~just enjoying each other.

When Quentin saw all the love and joy portrayed on Harry's picture- he just sobbed deeply and walked away to the restroom~~~leaving his lonely picture on the table. Harry picked it up and looked at it. It showed (crudely, of course) two older people, (older and bigger than Quentin at least) being very busy and laughing ----- with a little boy sitting all by himself sobbing, as tears fell on his artwork. He'd drawn chains on his ankles, and a picture of a heart as big as a sheet of paper that had been ripped into two pieces!

Un-be-known to Quentin; Dr. Toymann and Quentin's parents, Carl and Betty Numbsence had been watching the whole thing through a one-way mirrored window in his office. Harry took the picture to his dad; who showed it to Quentin's parents: then returned it to Harry so he could replace it before Quentin found it missing.

When Quentin returned; Harry met him with: "Hey, Quentin! You wanna meet my dad? He's a great guy! You'll love 'im! He really likes kids, I promise. I think he'll love you! You wanna? Huh? Huh?

"Okay!" said Quentin. "It might be nice to find an adult who might at least

TRY to listen to my heart—if mom and dad will let him!" Quentin thought.

"Bring your picture with you," said Harry; Dad loves pictures!

The two boys entered the office, where Harry cried out: "Dad! See my new friend? Isn't he GREAT!? You wanna see the great picture he drew of his family? I think he's just wonderful!!"

Quentin looked at Harry and his dad with eyes as wide with unbelief as saucers! "You do?" Quentin asked. "How come he thinks that? I don't believe him- cause I'm NOT, I'm bad and ugly." he thought to himself.

"Sure!" Harry said. "We had some fun together. I don't like talking to myself; but, we talked and drew pictures together. It was great fun, I thought. How 'bout you, Quentin?"

"Yes," thought Quentin. "I guess------------------------I know it was! Just to have someone spend

14

some time with just me. Just for me NOT to be invisable even for a little while! Yes, it WAS fun! Thank you, Harry! Thank you!!"

"Excuse me for just a moment. I need to ask Harry to do something for me - I'll be right back," said Dr. Toymann.

No one knew that this whole scene had been pre-arranged between Harry and his dad just to try to soften Quentin's protective shield and get at the root of the problem.

Chapter 4
THE LUNCHEON

When Dr. Toymann returned; he sent Quentin with Harry while he spoke again with Mr. And Mrs. Numbsense-finishing up the visit by making an appointment to talk with Quentin the following Wednesday informally at a luncheon he and Harry were going to prepare. "So, we can count on seeing the three of you at--say—12:30 pm on Wednesday, February 29th?" he asked.

"Sure, doctor---can we bring anything?" they inquired.

"No, tha---er—wait. Actually, that might be a great idea to keep it friendly and informal! Okay! How about some of Quentin's favorite homemade cookies? You can bring cookies! That would be great! Okay, see you on Wednesday." he said.

While Dr. Toymann was busy discussing plans with Quentin's parents; Harry was making an invitation with Quentin: "Say, Quentin; how'd you like to come over for lunch with dad and me next week? I'd love to have someone to have lunch with. Dad's a great dad, but, he's usually so busy during the day that we just kinda hurry through lunch so he can get back to work. You wanna come? I'm sure dad won't care!"

Quentin's eyes lit up like flood lights! "Wow! Could this actually be happening to him, Quentin Numbsense?! Someone had just invited him over for the first time in his life! How neat! How really cool was that?!" he thought. If only mom and dad would allow him to do this—this once—it would mean so much to him. "I'll have to ask my mom and dad—and—oh, I'll have to make sure your dad don't care if I come! That would be way cool, Harry! Thank you! -----Are you sure you want me to come? I'm younger than you, and I know there's a lot of boys closer to your age who would love to be your friend!?" Quentin asked.

"No!" Harry replied, "I want you, Quentin Numbsense, to be my friend! I like you, Quentin!"

"Okay, cool---way cool! THIS IS AWESOME!!!" shouted Quentin as he embraced his new friend with the biggest 'man-hug' he could muster.

The boys descended the stairs to return to the office; Quentin feeling lighter than air for the first time in his life. He finally had a friend---- something he'd prayed and cried for all of his life. "Would mom and dad let him keep this friend or continue to keep him locked up?" he wondered.

As the boys re-entered the office; Quentin's parents were 'shocked' to see the way their son's face lit up. He had such a big smile on his face that it almost seemed to divide his face into two pieces. What had happened to him? What had Harry done or said to him to bring about this drastic change in his countenance?

"Mommy, daddy; you'll never guess it!! Harry wants to be my friend! Harry wants to be MY FRIEND!!! Can I come to Harry's for lunch next week? Can I? Can I, please? Pretty please, can I? I won't ask for anything else if I can just have Harry as a friend mommy; I promise I won't, honest!?!"

Quentin's parents glanced over at Dr. Toymann, who just nodded and winked at them.

"Sure, Quentin- we can do that. Harry's dad has just invited us for lunch on Wednesday. We'll see you Wednesday at 12:30, Mr. Toymann. Looking forward to it. As they left Dr. Toymann's office they, too felt like a big weight had just been lifted off their backs. And Quentin—he was skipping and whistling all the way to the car— at least four feet ahead of them!!!

Back at the house, Quentin was almost too excited to eat. "But, Quentin, if you want to be well enough to have lunch with Harry next week you've got to keep your strength up", they told him.

"But mommy; I'm just TOO excited! I've finally got a friend—ME, Quentin Numbsense! How'd THAT happen? That's ALL I've ever wanted! I didn't think I'd EVER have a friend. I thought I was supposed to be by myself ALL my life. I thought that's why God put me here. Me Quentin-NOW HAS A FRIEND! YIPEE!!!"

After dinner was cleaned up, Quentin went to return to his video game; but mom and dad stopped him. "How about a family night?" they asked him. "We can play cards, draw, or play a board game; and then we'll eat popcorn and watch a movie! Does that sound like fun?"

"Whoa-what was this?" Quentin wondered. "Mom and dad never wanted a 'family night' before—what happened?" "This has been the coolest day of my life!" He thought to himself. "Sure, SURE!" he said.

While he and dad picked out a movie, mom busied herself making popcorn and koolaid for the movie. She also got some of Quentin's favorite cookies: TRIPLE CHOCOLATE CHOCOLCTE CHIP with nuts!

After the movie and a bubble bath, Quentin was tucked into bed—but found it hard to go to sleep, (although he was exhausted from his big exciting day). This day had been like a fairytale. Not only had he gotten a friend like he'd been waiting for—but he'd gotten his parents back! And to think that he thought that mom and dad's new friend was going to take them away from him. 'Why—he'd given them back to him—plus a new friend!! It had to be a dream—things like this just don't happen to Quentin Numbsense. Never! He sang himself to sleep that night.

When the sun arose the next morning, Quentin didn't want to wake up. He just 'knew' it was a dream he'd dreamed in the night. It couldn't be real—not for him. But sure enough when he got out of bed, there was mom and dad waiting in the kitchen to have breakfast with him. His favorite breakfast, too: chocolate chip pancakes with chocolate syrup, sausage, and orange juice. And as if that wasn't enough— dad had taken off from work just to be with him today, and mom had devoted the whole day to spending time with he and dad. "I must still be dreaming," he thought. But no---it was real!!!

Chapter 5
THE DAY

Time passed quickly and it was soon time to go for lunch at Harry's, (although to Quentin it seemed like a decade had passed-he just couldn't hardly wait—he was so-o-o excited!) Quentin was up and ready to go before sun up! Running into mom and dad's bedroom; he proceeded to try to wake them up. "Mommy, daddy, come on— wake up! We don't want to be late! Come on, hurry!" Quentin shouted.

"Calm down, son- the sun's not even awake yet!" They told him.

"I know---bu—well, we gotta get breakfast over with! And you'll want to make sure everything's cleaned up; and I wanna help you do that! Come on; I can't wait!"

"It's REALLY a little early yet, son. We have plenty of time yet---lunch isn't until 12:30 this afternoon; and if you're going to help us prepare, we'll be ready in plenty of time if we start-- say at least by 8am. It's only 5:30 now, son." "Well, I'm already dressed and can't sleep anymore in my bed right now. Whatta you want me to do, play my game? I can't, I don't want do. I can't even think about it now!!

"Why don't you climb up here with us for a couple of hours—then we'll get up and get started, okay? We don't want you to get sleepy at Harry's without being able to spend time with him; and you will be if you stay up now!" "Okay, thank you; mommy and daddy, thank you!"

Quentin climbed up between his mom and dad, and snuggled down under the covers---but found it almost impossible to close his eyes. He lay there quietly so as not to disturb his parents— staring at the ceiling—while visions of the upcoming adventure danced in his mind. What a fun day he was finally going to have!! This was one day he was sure that he'd NEVER forget! Never before had he imagined he'd EVER have fun with a friend like this!!

Quentin lay there for what seemed to be an eternity; (about 45 minutes), and finally drifted off to sleep.

When the day finally broke--- there was mom and dad jostling him and saying: "Come on, sleepyhead! Times a-wastin'!" Behind them he could smell the aroma of breakfast: bacon, toast, eggs, ---and what was that wonderful smell? Was it-- blueberry muffins? Wow! What a breakfast!" I hope I'll have room for lunch at Harry's!" Quentin thought. But those weren't the only smells radiating from the kitchen! What was that most tantalizing smell he could sense? It couldn't be---could it? "Oh! WOW! Double chocolate, chocolate chip cookies! My favorite—but why?"-he wondered.

After Quentin had redressed himself,
washed his face, and combed his hair;
he went skipping and whistling into the
kitchen. Mom already had breakfast on
the table and was pouring the juice.

"Mommy, are you making
my favorite cookie?

"Yes, Quentin. I thought they'd be
nice to take on our luncheon date at
Harry's, don't you?" answered mother.
"Yes, oh yes! I sure hope Harry likes the
same kind of cookie I do! This day is
going to be SO-O-O fun!! I can't wait!"

Quentin couldn't believe it---he was
so-o-o hungry for the first time in---
well---a long time. He gobbled so fast
that mom and dad had to tell him
to slow down so that he wouldn't
choke! He felt so famished.

After breakfast, mom and dad asked
Quentin if he could entertain himself
while they finished the cookies, cleaned
up the kitchen, and got dressed. (They
were still in their pajamas and robes).

Quentin retired to the living room and put on his PS3—but couldn't seem to get interested in it . "What can I do"? He thought. Then an idea hit him: "I'll make a 'Thank-You card for Harry and his dad for letting me come to lunch today! I've finally got my first friend! This is so-o-o great, and cool, and awesome!!! He said to himself." He sat down at his craft table and was very busy working on his 'Thank-You' card when mom and dad came into the room.

"Oh! Mommy and daddy, we can't go just yet; I'm not done making my card yet!"

"That's okay, son. You go ahead and finish. We've got coffee to finish and a few minutes before we leave."

"Great! This card has to be perfect!! Nothing but the best for MY friend!!!"

Mom and dad finished their morning coffee, took their cups to the kitchen, and returned to Quentin.

"Mommy and daddy, I'm done---do you think he'll like it?" he questioned.

"Yes, son, it's REALLY nice— I'm sure he'll like it!" dad said:" Are you ready to go?"

They headed for the car—then Quentin ran back to the house. "Mommy, you forgot the cookies---we gotta get the cookies!"

"Son, we took them out earlier---- they're already in the car, let's go!!"

Chapter 6
THE SURPRIZE

Upon arriving at Dr. Toymann's office, Quentin could hardly contain his excitement! Dr. Toymann had closed the office for the whole afternoon---just to work with Quentin and his parents. They were ushered upstairs by a receptionist who, after they arrived, locked up the office and went home.

Lunch was wonderful;--although all Quentin could think about was his new friendship. "Someone actually likes me — Quentin! How awesome!!!" He kept rehearsing to himself. Mom and dad talked a lot to Dr, Toymann; but Quentin didn't mind. After all; he still had his parents—and a friend. Everything was okay!

After lunch was over; Harry entered the room with a large wrapped box and set it down in front of Quentin. "Is this for me?" he asked Harry.

"Yes, Quentin. I have a favor to ask you. You see; I'm getting ready to go away to school—and—well—open the box, please."

Quentin tore open the box, but he didn't look happy while opening it. "What, Harry? You can't leave! I thought you wanted to be my friend? Friends don't move away from friends; if they're REALLY friends! How can you do this? I need you, Harry!!" Quentin exclaimed while tears streamed down his face.

"I know," Harry said; "I DO want to be your friend! I AM your friend! But... see—my school is starting up again in April and I really need to go. You see----I'm trying to learn how I can be a better friend to kids like you, Quentin. We can still write each other, and well;--I'm not leaving for a few more weeks yet. But I wanted you to have my dog to remember me by until I come back. His name is

Horace; but you can rename him, if you like. He's YOUR dog now. Okay?"

They exchanged manly hugs and promised to write each other (and to continue to be friends); then parted company. All the way home, Quentin remained quiet---not speaking a word—just hugging his new dog and sobbing Harry's name over and over.

When they arrived at home; mom and dad made a nice little bed for the dog, in Quentin's room, right next to his bed.

Chapter 7
A NEW BEGINNING

Quentin played with his dog all evening---even during the popcorn and movie mom and dad had prepared for him. Then mom and dad asked Quentin what he would name his new pet. "Are you going to call him Horace like Harry--or name him something else?"

Quentin thought for a moment, then announced: "His name is: - My Friend Harry!!" The start of a beautiful friendship!

After that day at the luncheon, life would never be the same. Quentin had 2 new friends, and 2 loving parents--- what more could he ask for? You would often see him in his back yard running and playing with his NEW FRIEND HARRY—as well as a cousin or two –and maybe even a neighborhood friend!!

Mom and dad were happy, too. After all, they had their smart, sweet little boy back---and didn't have to struggle with him anymore.

What an amazing power---- love and friendship?!!

Kirstin 6yrs old

Heidi 8yrs old

Chapter 8
BROKEN HOMES

Kirstin was a beautiful, 5 yr. old brunette girl with a problem. She didn't know who she was or who she was supposed to be. She lived alone with her father. Mom had run away with dad's best friend, Bob, when she was only 2 yrs. Old. She couldn't even hardly remember what mom looked like; unless she looked at the pictures of her that dad had locked up in his bedroom.

"Why had mom done that to them? Where was mom? Who was mom? Why didn't mommy love them anymore? Was it her fault? Was she such a bad little girl that it caused mommy to hate her and daddy? What could she have done?" Very bleak, depressing thoughts occupied Kirstin's mind continually.

Daddy was a good dad---she knew daddy loved her; but daddy was so-o-o-o lonely, and she knew it (although he tried not to let her see it)! Every once in a while, Kirstin would sneak into her dad's bedroom after he'd tucked her in bed for the night—thinking she was asleep. What would she find daddy doing---but watching old family videos of when she was first born—while he clenched a picture of him and a pretty lady in a wedding dress to his chest---with tears running down his face! Daddy was so lonely. Why had mommy and Bob done this? Did they hate them that much? Why? What had she and daddy done to cause this to happen?

Chapter 9
THE OBJECT OF ANGER

Two blocks away lived her 8 yr. old cousin, Heidi who also had her own set of problems: her dad was an alcoholic and didn't know (or care to know) how to treat her and her mother.

When he was sober—which was very seldom—he was wonderful! He could be so nice! He loved to barbeque outside for them on nice days when he was sober. On those occasions, they'd invite Kirstin and her dad down for dinner. Kirstin would help daddy fix a side dish and dessert. They were really fun times. (Probably the only time Kirstin would hear her daddy laugh. How she enjoyed those times!!) But Heidi's dad didn't stay sober for long—he had to have his beer and whiskey!

As Kirstin and her dad would leave the barbeque party at Heidi's; she would hear Heidi's dad yelling at Heidi and her mom. She even heard him on several occasions saying as he yelled: "What's wrong with you? Look at your stupid daughter! She must take after you because you're SO stupid!! Shut up--- the both of you! I can't stand your babbling and nagging!! Why isn't the house cleaned up yet? It should already be done! You idiots!!!---Why do I even try? You're worthless!!" Then he'd storm out of the house and go to the tavern; where he'd stay until closing time. He had beer in the house and whiskey in the garage, but that didn't matter—he didn't want to be home.

Heidi's dad had a good job that paid well---and her mom as well, she worked hard, too; (for little pay); but the money didn't last very long; so they also fought about finances. Mom would get ready for work and ask dad for a few dollars to gas up the car or to help with the bills, and dad would explode in a furious temper! So, mom would usually tell him to keep his money and try to take care of things herself; while dad drank up his money.

Even Christmas at their house was slim. Mom would do what she could, but when she asked dad to help; he'd explode into a rage, and pick up as little as he could get by with (usually underclothes and socks were his norm—if THAT much!) He did help get groceries for them: but, they had to eat whatever HE wanted to eat—they DIDN'T get a choice!) It was HIS way— or NO way: they didn't have a voice!

Chapter 10
LIFE WITHOUT LOVE

These girls felt very trapped in a life that was really NO LIFE—just a painful existence! Why had God dealt them this kind of life? They both really loved their parents—but were powerless to change anything for the better. Every time they tried to help, things just got worse!

Heidi and Kirstin spent as much time together as they could; as much as their parents would allow them to. Heidi had quite a few responsibilities to attend to that her dad had delegated to her (which he expected to be done on his time table- or punishment and cursing ensued)! Then; if he was drinking, he wouldn't allow her to leave the house or have anyone over. It wasn't that he wanted time with her, he just didn't want to hear laughter in the house. Heidi and her mom (Maurene) spent a lot of time together in the kitchen or Heidi's bedroom. (Heidi wasn't allowed in dad's bedroom unless she was ill---and even then she had to knock and announce her need before entering!) It was literal 'prison on earth' as Heidi's mom called it!!

Life to these two girls was like a hopeless trap!! They'd see other children at home or school--- playing, laughing, and seemingly enjoying life; but their lives seemed entrenched in loneliness, sadness, and fear. What made them so different from other people?

Chapter 11
LIVING THE PAST

Of course, Jerry, Heidi's dad,
hadn't always been this way!

Heidi could remember the happy
times before her aunt Sandy, Kirstin's
mother and her dad's only sister, ran
away. Those were REALLY happy times!
They would all get together once a
week (usually EVERY Friday night).
What fun they'd have together: playing
games and watching TV together!
They'd take turns hosting the evening.
One Friday it'd be at Heidi's house,
and the next Friday at Kirstin's. Now
those days were long gone. Would
they EVER see happy times again?

Daddy had started drinking right after
Aunt Sandy left; and now all the good
times were gone with her. Why had she
done that? Didn't she care about ANY
of them? And poor little Kirstin- just

a baby when Aunt Sandy left. What a horrible thing to happen to a baby?!

Heidi's dad had almost lost his mind when Aunt Sandy left. That's why (he said) he had to have his liquor – to keep his sanity! But it sure didn't seem to be doing anything good for him. There HAD to be another way, one that might ACTUALLY help! That would be great! If only they could find a way –maybe the two families could find a way to be happy again.

They hadn't heard from Aunt Sandy since she left – three years ago. That's why Uncle Tommy was so sad and daddy was so angry. Why hadn't she sent any of them a card-or anything- in THREE years? Had she been able to forget all about them? How ---- and why? Was there ANY way she could get ahold of Aunt Sandy—ANYTHING she could do to let Sandy know just how her leaving had messed up everyone's life? Would Aunt Sandy even care?

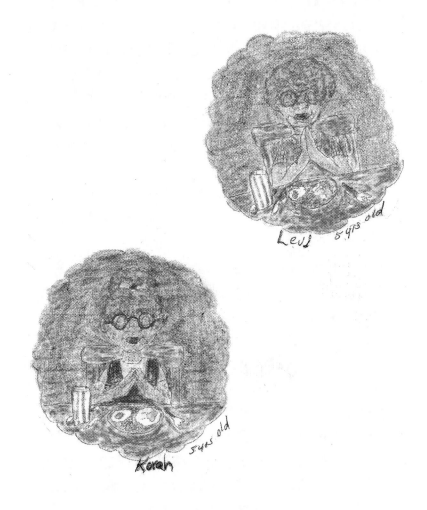

Levi   5 yrs old

Korah   5 yrs old

Chapter 12
THE TWINS

It was a nice, peaceful Saturday morning. Korah and Levi (twins) with their brother Jeremy and mother Maggie were at 'GOD'S HOUSE' where they attended regularly. Only today was different. Today they were being instructed in how to plant 'WORD SEEDS'—as Pastor Higgenbotham called it. Mother had started them attending this fun church as soon as daddy's funeral had ended a year and a half ago.

Anyway, they were learning exciting, fun ways to invite others to Sunday school, and couldn't hardly wait to get started!

At 12:15 pm Pastor "Higgy", as the twins called him, prayed and dismissed everyone to the fellowship hall for lunch: where they'd pray, split up

into families (teams of three or four),
and canvas the neighborhood.

After lunch, mother took Jeremy and
the twins and was given Resurrection
Blvd, to canvas. How they loved talking
to other people about how to be happy!

Even though daddy had died with a
massive stroke followed by a heart
attack after completing his chemo
treatment for lung cancer---mom
and Jeremy had managed to not
only keep them together- but, also
to help them realize they'd truly
get to see daddy again and that
he was looking out for them! They
were happy in spite of their loss!

Chapter 13
THE INVITE

As they started down Resurrection Boulevard; the first place they found someone home was Heidi Lipscomb's house. And; as God would have it- daddy had gone to get his car checked out! He'd probably stop to buy more liquor before coming home: so Heidi and her mom, Maurene, could visit for a while. (Just not TOO long.)

Maggie and the children were welcomed in with glasses of lemonade and freshly baked muffins.

As Maggie and the children spoke to them about how to find happiness; Heidi and her mother sat spellbound! After Korah, Levi, Jeremy, and Maggie finished explaining about the peace, joy, and fun at their church; they asked them if they'd like to join them (they'd

have the bus pick them up) unless
they wanted to carpool with them.

"We'll think about it- we promise!
Probably not this week because of dad-
but we'll try to make it next week. Who
do we call?" Maurene asked them.

They exchanged phone numbers
and promised to call them
later on in the week.

"Okay, we'll be praying for you." Said
Ms. Tilton and the children, and left.

Chapter 14
THE SUNDAY HORROR

Later that evening, daddy
finally arrived back home.

"What did they tell you about
the car, Jerry?" Maurene asked
daddy. "You were gone so long- is
everything okay with the car?"

"Nag, nag, nag- there you go again,"
said daddy. "Not that it's any of YOUR
business; but the car's fine. I ran into
a couple of friends at the shop, and
we stopped in for a drink. Are you
happy now, mother?" daddy said very
sarcastically. "I feel like I'm living
with my mother—you want me to write
out an itinerary for you, mom? Can't
a guy have a little time to himself
without being hassled about HIS
time? Do I ask what you do all day?"

Chapter 15
IS GOD REAL?

Daddy stormed through to the kitchen. What? Where's dinner?? I don't see anything here; but--- WHAT'S THIS? ---- six glasses and six plates. And one of the glasses has lipstick on it! Are you having parties behind my back? Who you been messin' with, Maurene? And in front of MY daughter!! What an unexpected DISAPPOINTMENT you've turned out to be!!! I can't even trust you long enough to get my car looked at! Who WERE they, Maurene?? Now don't try to lie to me because I have ways of finding out whether or not you're involved in an affair! Tell me now, you little cheater; tell me the truth!"

"Daddy, daddy!" Heidi interrupted with tears streaming down her face. "It wasn't a party, honest. Korah and Levi came by with their big brother and mother to talk to us about going to...." She stopped talking and looked at dad as he whipped around to stare her into the face.

"Going where? Who in the world is Korah and Levi? Where do you know them from? What do they have to do with any of this? Come on, fess up! Are you turning out to be like your mother?" dad shouted at her.

Korah and Levi go to my school. They're twins. They just asked us if we wanted to go to Sunday school with them. That's all—I promise!" Heidi said.

Mom stood behind him, shaking her head. (She had intended to talk to dad about the issue when he sobered up in the morning—but Heidi had already spilled the beans. Now all they had to do was wait for the storm they knew that they'd see. What a life? What a lonely, fearful life?

Chapter 16
THE STORM

Dad left the kitchen in a huff--- then quickly returned. "Oh, no—you're NOT going to get religion on me! NO!! I forbid you to go- tomorrow.......or EVER!!! It's hard enough staying here with the two WORTHLESS people you've become; YOU DEFINITELY ARE NOT GOING TO GET GOD NOW!!! If you do; I'll be forced to take action. I'll sue the church for ruining my family--- and if that don't work: I'll commit suicide and then implicate the church!" (That'll stop 'em!-he thought) Then he passed out on the sofa.

Heidi ran to Maurene and cried heart-wrenching tears into her mother's apron. "What'll we do, mom?" she asked. "Will we EVER be happy and not afraid again? Does God even care about us? Is there even a God for real?

Korah, Levi, Jeremy, and Maggie looked so happy. Was that just an act?"

Dad had told them ever since Aunt Sandy left that there was: NO God! NO heaven, NO hell---there's just us. We live, we die, and go to dust. That's all life was. It had no REAL purpose!"

Daddy just HAD to be wrong—there just HAD to be more to life than that!! After all, other people looked happy—why couldn't they be? Was God partial? Who was He? Did He REALLY exist—or was it just a pipe dream? Heidi just HAD to find out. There just HAD to be some help for them out there---there just HAD to be!!!!!

Chapter 17
THE ACCIDENT

Well, as you might guess, they didn't go to Sunday school—they were afraid of what dad might do.

Dad's anger problem didn't stop with the weekend—his drinking either. After he finally woke up Sunday afternoon, he stormed through the house and out to the garage.

'I've just got to think! I've just got to find a way to get everybody to LEAVE US ALONE!" he shouted after entering the garage and downing half of a fifth of Jack Daniels.

Dad stayed in the garage all afternoon, drinking. When Maurene went to get him for dinner; she found him passed out on the garage floor with a crowbar laying above his head. Upon looking around she found that two windows of her car had been broken; the left rear fender was caved in; and one of her tires had been split through to the belt. Jerry's head was cut and bleeding.

She ran into the house, grabbed the phone and a clean white cloth; and ran out to put pressure on Jerry's head while she proceeded to call 911.

Heidi saw mom running and followed after her. "Oh, no, daddy! Mommy, what's happened to daddy?" she questioned as tears flooded her eyes.

"He's gotten himself so crazy drunk that he's hurt himself." Maurene said as she placed the emergency call.

Within no time (although it seemed like it took forever), the paramedics arrived. They assessed his condition and determined that his blood pressure had gotten out of control and caused him to stroke out. When he fell, the crowbar had hit his head causing deep contusions right above his eyes, slicing his left eyebrow in half. They bandaged Jerry's head and transported Him to Whispering Heights Trauma Center for further evaluation and admittance.

Maurene called Tom; and she and Heidi rushed to the hospital. Tom and Kirstin met them there.

"What happened, Maurene?" asked Tom. "What happened?"

"He'd been out on another binge yesterday. While he was gone, a couple of the girl's schoolmates and their family came by to invite us to Sunday school. When Jerry returned last night, he found a glass with lipstick on it and turned into a wild man (calling us worthless cheaters), then we thought that would be the end of that episode—but; lo, and behold— when he woke up this afternoon, he returned to the garage and started drinking again. When I went to call him for supper; I found him unconscious on the floor with a blood-stained crowbar near his head. He tore up my car and passed out--- or stroked out. The crowbar must've hit him pretty good when he fell! I found three empty fifths of Jack on the floor along with two quart beer bottles. I don't know if he's going to make it! What are we going to do if he doesn't? He wasn't always like this! I remember the good times...I just don't know how to bring them back again! What'll we do?

The two girls were huddled in a corner of the waiting room; crying so hard it seemed they couldn't breathe!!

Chapter 18
DIAGNOSIS

After what seemed an eternity (about 1 ½ hours); the doctor came into the waiting room. "Mrs. Lipscomb!" he called. Maurene approached the doctor. "How is he? Will he be alright?" she asked. "What's wrong with him?"

Alcohol poisoning and liver damage. He's not awake- but you can see him briefly. We're going to keep him for further tests and treatment. He'll be on CCU in room 6."

Heidi ran up to go in with her mother; but Maurene asked her to wait with Uncle Tom and let her go in first because 'daddy wouldn't be able to talk right now.'

When Maurene approached where Jerry lay, she gasped: Help us; oh Lord! He's so pale and- why is his coloring so yellow? This wasn't Jerry! It just couldn't be!!"

The doctor assured her that it was Jerry, and that they would do all they could to speed his recovery—they just weren't making any guarantees at this time.

On Tuesday afternoon Maurene received a phone call. It was Maggie wanting to know if there was anything they could do." All I know right now is you can pray for Jerry--- for us---if you will. I don't know if he'll pull through or not; and I don't even know how to reach his sister with the news. Things are such a mess right now. I "don't know if I'm coming or going. What'll we do if he doesn't make it?"

Chapter 19
HELP IS ON THE WAY

"We sure will pray. And don't worry: - the God we serve specializes in the impossible! Just have faith! Would you like us to pick up Heidi tomorrow night so you can have time without worrying after her? We're having a special 'family night' at church and it might be good for Heidi to be away from the trauma for a while. We'll have her home by 8 o'clock!" Maggie offered.

"Sure, that would be great! She's been through SO much for a little girl. Maybe I'll be able to have time to try to locate Jerry's sister. She's the only family he has left. Thank you. What time does she need to be ready to go?"

"We'll be there by 5:30, if that's not too early...and don't worry about dinner; we eat at church."

"Oh, no- that'll be fine. I can
have her ready by that time.
Thank you! Thank you!!"

When Heidi returned from school,
Maurene told her about the invitation.

"But mom, I wanted to be
with you to help with Kirstin.
What's Kirstin gonna do?"

Maurene hadn't thought about that. "I'll
call Uncle Tom and see if Kirstin can go
with you. Would that be okay, Heidi?"

"Yes, I guess so. But are you and
Uncle Tom gonna be alright?"

"Yes, we'll be fine. We're gonna
try to find Aunt Sandy while you
girls are at church, okay?"

"Aunt Sandy? Yes, oh yes, that would
be great, mom! I've been praying and
hoping we could find her! Do you think
we can? Do you think she'll come
home, mom? That would be great!
Maybe we could all be happy again!

Okay mom; if Kirstin goes, I'll go."
Maurene proceeded to fix supper.

After they finished eating, Heidi
went to finish her homework.
Maurene put the dishes to soak, and
picked up the phone to call Tom.

"Tom, Heidi's been invited to a family
night at 'God's House' tomorrow. How
about letting Kirstin come over and
go with her? You and I can maybe
use that time to try to reach Sandy
with the news about Jerry. She really
needs to know about it! Okay?"

"Okay, Maurene. I'll bring her over right
after she gets home from school. I'm
off tomorrow afternoon, so I'll bring a
pizza for our dinner. Don't worry 'bout
fixing anything to eat, okay?" Tom said.

"Maggie told me that they'd be feeding
the girls at church tomorrow—some
kind of special dinner of some sort."

Chapter 20
PEACE IN THE MIDST OF A STORM

Wednesday morning Maurene called Maggie to get an okay for Kirstin to go along. "Sure, the more the merrier!" Maggie exclaimed. "We'll see you at 5:30."

Kirstin and Heidi got home and worked on homework together. Just about the time they were finishing there was a knock on the door. Heidi ran to answer it.

"Heidi! You and your cousin ready?" inquired Korah and Levi. "Yes, we'll be right out;—and oh—her name is Kirstin- Kirstin Newsome!"

As the girls got ready to go out the door; Tom and Maurene grabbed them and gave them a big squeeze and kiss---wishing them a fun time at church. "We'll do our best to find Sandy!" they affirmed.

When the girls arrived at church; Korah and Levi took them by the hand and led them toward a nice-looking older man. "Pastor Higgy!" they called out." These are our friends Heidi and her cousin Kirstin that we told you about from our Team Evangelism Day!"

"Hello, and welcome to "God's House!" Pastor Higgenbotham told them. "If you need ANYTHING or have ANY questions, feel free to ask. After all, 'God's House' is YOUR house!"

"Wow--- this man was nice; but he wasn't dressed like a pastor. As a matter of fact; NO ONE was dressed like church people were usually dressed. What WAS this place? Pastor was wearing a blue plaid cowboy shirt and blue jeans. Everyone else had on casual clothes (no dresses or slacks and----TENNIS SHOES!!) They weren't used to seeing church like this!

Everyone gathered into this large room with 12 long white tables. At the front of the room was a large counter filled with homemade chili and crackers, peanut butter sandwiches 3 Or 4 different types of dessert, tea, coffee, and lemonade. WOW! What a feast?!

'Pastor Higgy', as he was called, got up in front of the group and proceeded to say the blessing:

"Dear Lord; we humbly beseech YOU today to bless this food for which we give YOU innumerable thanks for providing. We ask that YOU nourish and fill our bodies (and souls) with what we need to keep us strong, healthy, and on fire for You, Lord. And we thank YOU for sending our new sisters; Heidi and Kirstin to us, Father. We ask that YOU be with them; giving them Your peace and joy like they've never experienced before. And bring them (and their families) back to be a constant part of us. In Jesus' (our brother's) Name, Amen.

Heidi and Kirstin couldn't hold back the tears. They hadn't felt love like this for a long time. They could sense SOMEONE there that wasn't visible to the naked eye; and they felt HIS loving touch on their hearts.

As soon as dinner was over; they all divided and went into different age groups, meeting in different rooms. The girls remained with Korah and Levi.

Once in the meeting room, they expected like a typical Sunday school lesson- but it wasn't at all like that! They were taught interactive action games—that taught Christ-like principles—on everything from giving your heart to Jesus, to learning how to deal with (and overcome) anger issues. This lasted for about 1 & 1/2hours.

After being dismissed from learning time; adults and children gathered together in one large room filled with chairs for worship time. But even this wasn't what they expected! Adults and children all gathered together in one large room filled with chairs—while the teenagers and young people gathered in front of the gathering to help everyone learn to illustrate with actions—the songs that Pastor Higgy sang. The actions were displayed on a movie screen behind them and pastor. After about thirty or forty-five minutes, Pastor Higgy led the group in prayer, and everyone went home. The girls were truly pumped and excited. They decided they wanted to try to talk their parents into coming on Sunday. Pastor Higgy took the girls home so he could talk to their parents.

While all this was going on, Tom and Maurene were having their own problems. They couldn't seem to locate Sandy anywhere! It was like she had just disappeared from the face of the earth!! After leaving Tom, she had remarried. They tried EVERY phone book, statewide directory, and emergency helpline—trying to locate Bob Massey's or Cassandra Massey's name; but to NO avail. Of all things- either they had an unlisted number or didn't even have a phone. How were they going to find her? They just HAD to find her soon-or it might be too late! But how??

Pastor Higgenbotham walked the girls to the door of Heidi's house and rang the doorbell just as the girls rushed in the front door.

"Mom, Uncle Tom—Pastor Higgy wants to see you. He's at the door."

"Well, ask him to come in girls. Don't leave him standing out there---that's rude."

The girls led Pastor Higgy inside. He extended his hand to Maurene and Tom: "Dunstyn Higgenbotham- I hope I'm not interrupting anything important! I just wanted to meet you and let you know what wonderful children you have – and to see if I can be of any help to you. I understand, Mrs. Lipscomb, that your husband is in Whispering Heights. Is there any way I can be of help? Would it be alright for me to pay him a visit?"

"Thank you, Pastor Higgenbotham that would be real nice. He's chemically unconscious right now; so he won't be able to speak to you—which is probably good---seeing as the church invitation from Mrs. Tilton is what set him off before this happened. Yes, Pastor, I'd love for you to pay him a visit —and maybe pray for him. I don't know if he's going to make it through this; and certainly don't want him to leave here without making it right. He wasn't always like this—just these last 3 years or so (since, well, uh- I won't bore you with details.) Thank you, Pastor, thank you!"

"That's quite alright, Mrs. Lipscomb. You're quite welcome. It's what I do- and I love doing it! And by the way; just call me 'Higgy'- everybody else does. I guess my name is easier to pronounce that way! Hope to see you in service soon; and I'll be praying for your search results. Please let us know if we can be of help with anything. Here's my name and address. Good day! May God bless you and your

loved ones" he said as he handed
them a card and turned to leave.

Tom and Kirstin gave hugs and
kisses, picked up their things
and left for home. "We'll be back
to help find Sandy again in the
morning. Don't start without us;
okay?" (School was out for teacher
workshops on Thursday and Friday.)

"Okay, I'll fix breakfast for us tomorrow
since you bought dinner today, okay?"
Maurene called to Tom, who had waved
at her as he and Kirstin loaded into the
car. Back at the house, Tom had a new
problem: Kirstin was so joyous that she
almost appeared hyper!" Daddy, can
I go back again? Can I? Can I? I had
a so fun time, daddy! And they really
liked me, daddy; they REALLY did!
I was a little afraid because I didn't
know anyone except Korah and Levi;
but they helped me fit right in! I didn't
feel lonely at all! Can I, huh, can I?"

"We'll talk about this tomorrow. Right
now let's get your bath over with and

get you to bed. Tomorrow is breakfast at Heidi's and I don't think you'll want to be too sleepy to eat, do you? Here; Aunt Maurene gave me some of Heidi's favorite bubble bath for you. You wanna try some tonight?"

"Yeah, sure, okay! What kind is it, daddy?"

"Let's see—it says here: lavender and chamomile."

"What's that mean, daddy? What's lavender and chamomile mean, daddy?"

"Lavender and chamomile are special fragrances that come from pretty flowers. Maurene says that it helps Heidi rest when she's having trouble."

"Ok, ok! I'll try it because tonight I'm almost too happy and excited to sleep. Do you think it'll help me?"

"We'll certainly find out, won't we? Now, don't forget to wash

your hair and behind your ears
where sweat hides, okay?"

"Ok, daddy."

Kirstin stayed in that bubble bath
until after it cooled down—so long, in
fact that Tom began to worry. "Are you
okay in there, Kirstin? You've never
stayed in there that long before!"

"Yes, daddy. I really like this—it smells
so pretty that I don't want to stop
smelling it. Will I smell like lavender
and chamomile when I get out, daddy?"

"I don't know, Kirstin---but don't
let it get too cold. You might
catch a cold if you do, okay?"

"Okay, daddy. I'll be out in a little
while, don't worry; I'm okay!"

Another 10-15 minutes and
Kirstin was out and ready for
bed: but, where was Tom?

After searching the whole house; Kirstin found Tom in his usual place after he'd put her to bed---in his room with picture and home movie doing his usual thing (crying and calling mommies' name over and over-"Sandy, Sandy. Why Sandy? Where are you? We need you? Oh, Sandy!") His shirt collar was already damp with the tears he'd cried.

Chapter 21

Kirstin ran up to Tom's lap, wrapped her little arms around his neck, and cried with him. "Don't worry. Daddy. You and Aunt Maurene will find her soon. I know you will! Pastor Higgy's whole church prayed for us and said that if we just believe in Jesus and His love after we pray, that Jesus will work for us- and NO ONE CAN HIDE FROM HIM CAUSE HE KNOWS AND SEES EVERYTHING!! If we ask Him to; He'll show us where she is-or- He'll tell us how to find out! Heidi and I prayed all the way home from church that you'd find her—so; I KNOW you will!!! Just trust Jesus, daddy, okay? It'll be alright. I KNOW it will! Can I sleep in here tonight? I promise I'll be quiet and won't keep you awake!"

"Sure, Kirstin. That would be nice. Maybe with you here daddy might be able to settle down and get to sleep. Goodnight, sweetheart. I love you." Tom said as he and Kirstin embraced each other and cried.

"Love you, too, daddy." And Kirstin was fast asleep.

Chapter 22
NEW HOPE

Thursday morning arrived with a noisy surprise: the doorbell woke the sleepy duo up with a jolt at about 8am.

"Who could be at our door already this morning?" pondered the two of them as they put their robes on and went to the door.

When they opened the door they were surprised to see Pastor Higgenbotham. "I hope I didn't startle you. May I talk with you for a moment?" he asked.

"Well, I guess. If you promise to forgive us for not being dressed yet. Kirstin is off from school; and I took the day off because of my brother-in-law's condition: to help his wife with things. I haven't been up long enough to even fix coffee. Would you like some juice, pastor?"

"No, that's fine. I just stopped by to offer my help in any capacity your family might need it. Heidi told me about the problem you're dealing with last night. I thought I'd drop by and offer to help you locate her aunt; and maybe pick her up for you once she's been located. Please understand; I'm NOT trying to butt my nose in your business- I'm just offering to help you in ANY way I can. Please feel free to call me anytime. I'm a full-time pastor, so don't worry about interfering with my work schedule. I'm in the 'Soul's Business' exclusively. Nothing gets in the way of helping others. After all; Jesus calls us friends- and friends DO help each other, right?" (John 15:15-17)

"Well, that's really nice of you, Pastor! I'll be sure and let Maurene know. That's REALLY nice. Thank you."

"It's what I do- no thanks needed by me. God is the One who called and commissioned me to do this- thank Him! And by the way- just call me Dunstyn. Please keep me posted (if

you will) on things. The whole church
will be praying for all of you. Okay?"

"Okay! Thank you, Dunstyn, thank you."

Tom and Kirstin quickly showered,
dressed, and brushed their teeth.
They could hardly wait to get to
Heidi and Maurene. This morning
had started different and they
just knew that something was
going to break for them today!

As they arrived at Heidi's house,
they noticed a new spring in their
steps. They finally had hope!

Chapter 23
MYSTERY CALLER

Upon entering the living room, they suddenly became very hungry from the aromas coming from the kitchen. Maurene had prepared a really great breakfast: Belgian waffles with butter and maple syrup, and little link sausages. To complete the meal, they saw cups of coffee, juice glasses, and glasses of cold milk. Yum-yum!

As they were finishing up breakfast-the phone started ringing, so Heidi rushed to answer it. "Mom, it's some man who says he's with the Red Cross. He wants to speak to you!"

"Good morning, this is Mrs. Lipscomb. May I help you?"

"Yes, Mrs. Lipscomb. This is Marvin Newbomb. I'm with the Area Red Cross. We understand that you're trying to locate a---let's see---Sandra Newsome Massey. Is that right?"

"Yes, Mr. Newbomb. Her brother is in Whispering Heights Trauma Center in very critical condition, and we can't find a listing for her anywhere! She's his only other living relative!"

"That's why I'm calling you, Mrs. Lipscomb, we've located her. She's in Whaling, Mississippi. Would you like us to contact her for you?"

"Yes, that would be wonderful! Thank you!!" said Maurene. "God bless you!!"

She hung up the phone and tried to tell the others the news as tears flooded her face.

"What's the matter, mom? Is it daddy?" questioned Heidi.

Maurene grabbed a damp washcloth and wiped her face- took a deep breath- And proceeded to explain the nature of the mysterious caller

80

"No, honey- it wasn't about your dad. That nice man was calling to let us know that they've found your Aunt Sandy and-and---"she said through tears- "they're even going to contact her for us!!!!" Heidi and Kirstin beamed from ear to ear as they danced around the room. "We told you that Pastor Higgy and his church prayed for us and said that God would help us if we'd just trust Jesus! And He did, didn't He?"

"Yes! I guess He did!" Tom and Maurene emphatically stated.

Chapter 24
GOD PROVIDES

Tom and Kirstin spent the whole day with Heidi and Maurene. Somehow, the heavy weight seemed so much lighter! Although Jerry was still in VERY critical condition—now, there was a glimmer of hope. Someone had found Sandy, and was going to get the message of Jerry's condition to her. Who knows? This might be just what Jerry needed to pull through and be himself again! Could this be the answer to their prayers? Maybe!!

The four of them loaded into Tom's SUV, and headed for the hospital. "Should we tell daddy that we've found Aunt Sandy? That would REALLY make him happy, mommy!" Asked Heidi.

"For sure; that would make him happy; but, let's wait until she's home- let her surprise him. After all, they haven't talked to her yet. Let's make sure that she'll be here before we tell daddy. If we tell him and she doesn't show up, he'll think that we lied to him: and that could finish him off! Let's wait until we're sure, okay?" Maurene cautioned.

"Okay, mom, you're right, as usual. I'll keep the secret." promised Heidi, although it was the hardest thing she'd ever have to do. Her excitement was really hard, (almost impossible) to contain!

Tom and Maurene approached the GGU, when the girls asked if they'd be able to see Jerry this time. "Maybe. Let us go in first to make sure it's alright; then we'll take you in, okay? Did you girls bring anything to occupy yourselves with while we're in there?" they asked.

"Yes, we've got our pocket games. We'll be alright, mom. I'll look after Kirstin, okay? Don't be too long, though; because we want to see him, too. Okay?" answered Heidi

About 10 or 15 minutes later, they returned to the waiting room to talk to the girls. "There's really been no change yet. He's still asleep. We'll take one of you in at a time; because we don't want either of you to be frightened. He doesn't look like himself. Okay Heidi?" called Maurene. "You and I will go in first. Then we'll let Uncle Tom and Kirstin see him, okay?"

When Maurene and Heidi approached Jerry's bed, Heidi let out a loud {gasp}. "Mommy, why does daddy look so weird- what have they done to him? You were right—he sure DOESN'T look like my dad! Will they be able to bring daddy back? Oh, daddy!!!!" and broke into tears, as she threw herself on Jerry to give him a hug, "We love you---we ALL love you, daddy. Please get well and come home so we can be happy again, PLEASE!!!"

She was weeping uncontrollably; so Maurene thought she needed to take her out of Jerry's room and try to calm her down, {although it was all she could do to keep from crying herself}. 'Being a parent never was easy- but this event almost had made it unbearable!' she thought to herself as she ushered Heidi back to the waiting room.

Now it was Tom and Kirstin's turn. "Hold on tight to her, Tom," warned Maurene, "I thought Heidi was going to pass out when she saw him!"

Tom held Kirstin's hand. "I will, I promise." He said, as they entered the unit.

As they approached Jerry's room, tension was mounting. When Kirstin saw her uncle's still and silent body, she ran to her dad with her hand over her mouth: "Daddy, I'm getting sick"; she exclaimed; and with that she ran out of the room toward the waiting room- to try to make it to the restroom. Tom followed close behind her, but wasn't able to keep up with her. When he got to the exit door of the unit; Kirstin stood there crying and red-faced. "I'm SO sorry, daddy. I tried to get to the restroom- REALLY I DID- but it wouldn't wait!" Right inside the door was a pool of vomit. "I'm SO sorry, daddy- I tried to stop it, I promise! What's wrong with Uncle Jerry? He looks SO scary!"

"Uncle Jerry is real sick, honey. Don't worry about the mess-I'll get a nurse to get it cleaned up. After all, it WAS an accident. They'll understand."

Then they walked back to the nurse's desk to report the emesis accident.

"I'm SO sorry I messed up your pretty floor. I really tried to get to the bathroom in time- but it wouldn't wait! I'm sorry!" Kirstin told the nurse.

"Why does my Uncle Jerry look so scary?" she asked the nurse. "That's what made me throw up!" The nurse looked at Tom, nodded, and placed the call to housekeeping for the clean-up. "I think daddy needs to talk to you about that." She said, and went to place a caution sign at the unit door.

Tom and Maurene thought that that was enough drama for the girls for one day; so they decided to take them home and try to find a way to ease their minds.

Chapter 25
THE CHANGE

The following day, after the girls left for school, Tom and Maurene went back to the hospital. Jerry was still unconscious, but his coloring was a little better. He was muttering one word over and over again; so they called for medical personnel to help them understand the change.

"He's not awake, but keeps repeating that one word over and over Can you help us understand what he is trying to say?" Maurene asked the nurse.

As Maurene and Tom returned to Jerry's room with the nurse and doctor on call they were surprised to see Jerry's eyes open—although he still seemed to be out of it. He was still trying to talk.

The nurse and doctor bent down to check his vital signs and examine him further when they heard these syllables: "Sandimoridy, sandimoridy!" They related what they understood to his waiting family.

"It really doesn't make any sense- just inaudible jibberish. But, he is stable and it seems like he's trying to wake up. Would you folks have any idea what he might be meaning to say? That's really all we understood him say. We're sorry we couldn't be of more help." And they returned to their stations. "If there are any other changes- OF ANY KIND-please call us IMMEDIATELY!"

"Sandimoidy? That's what they heard? They're right—it DOES sound like jibberish! What could he be saying? That's NOT like him!!"

When they returned to Jerry's room, they found him quiet again and fast asleep. Not wanting to disturb his rest, they decided they should just call it a day and head home to solve the surprise of the mystery jibberish; so, after checking with the doctor, they returned home.

Chapter 26
CODE BLUE

The week went by without much change; although Jerry's frequent momentary consciousness and jibberish provided some relief and hope for the worried families.

The weekend seemed to be one of the hardest these families had faced since the accident. Jerry had taken a sudden turn for the worse. Code Blue was called in Jerry's room at 3:40am on an early spring day in March 1990 and—all of a sudden—doctors and nurses seemed to appear from out of the woodwork. The families were called in; and the girls were so frightened that they thought they were going to die, too. (Their little hearts were beating so hard that they thought their chests would explode!) They'd never seen so many doctors and nurses in one place before! Were there still people to care for the other patients in the hospital; or were they ALL with Jerry? What was happening? Would Jerry make it and come home- or was he dying? They couldn't bear the thought of losing Jerry without being able to let him know that they still loved him. The girls tried to burst through the unit doors to tell Jerry how they felt— but were ushered back to the waiting room. They ran to their parents crying so hard that they couldn't breathe.

"He's just gotta make it! He CAN'T die---he just CAN'T!!" They threw themselves on their parent's necks and screamed out: "Oh, God! You've just gotta let him live—we don't want to be here without him!! He's just gotta be alright—he's just gotta!! Help him, Jesus. Please help him!"

After about thirty minutes a doctor came out to talk to the family. "We've finally got a pulse and heartbeat. With your permission, Mrs. Lipscomb, we'd like to put him on a respirator. He still needs help to continue breathing; but that's up to you. Discuss it with you family and get back with us ASAP. He's resting right now---we've sedated him again to keep him from thrashing himself about and causing more labored breathing." Then he turned to leave.

"Doctor, we really don't have to discuss this---I believe that we all feel the same way. His sister is on her way from Mississippi, and I believe seeing her could do quite a bit to usher in his recovery. Anything you need to do to keep him with us---at least until Sandy arrives---you have our blessing. Right everybody?"

"Definitely!" said Tom

"He CAN'T die yet!" cried the girls.

"Daddy, why?" sobbed Heidi

Chapter 27
THE HEART SURPRISE

After they hooked Jerry up to the respirator; the doctor returned to talk to the families. "He's resting now; and his vital signs have stabilized. There's nothing more at this point that you folks can do for him. Why don't you go and try to get some rest—you all look like you could use some.

"No, mommy! I don't want to leave yet. Daddy's not awake yet, and I've just got to talk to him. I haven't told him that I still love him, mom. If he dies...." Said Heidi through a veil of tears, "he'll think that I'm still mad at him and that I don't love him anymore. He can't die believing that! He just CAN'T!!"

"It looks like you really have your work cut out for yourself, mom." The kindly doctor said as he bent down to whisper into Maurene's ear. "I can give you something to help her relax-and: if you like—maybe if she had something of her dad's to hold on to until he's rallied; it might help. Can you think of anything she might like to hold on to for her dad?"

"Well," said Maurene. "Jerry always wears a cross chain. He NEVER takes it off. Maybe if you could get that for her; it might help." She whispered to the doctor. "Okay. Will do, Mrs. Lipscomb."

"Mommy, mommy! Can daddy have my heart necklace?" Heidi asked-tugging at the plastic heart pendant that was fastened around her neck. "It's big enough that he'll be able to see it good when he wakes up---then he'll know that I gave it to him, and that I still love him! Can he, mommy?"

Maurene looked at the doctor who had just started to leave the waiting room.

"Maybe we can swap necklaces with him---would that be alright? He really doesn't need two necklaces on right now. That might cause him to strangle."

And with that he left the room with Heidi's plastic heart necklace in his hand.

In about fifteen minutes he returned. "Miss Heidi," he said. "I believe your dad would like for you to hold onto this for him until he gets home. What do you think?"

"Yes, oh yes!" shouted Heidi. "The cross necklace that you and me gave him on his birthday three years ago, mom! I'll never let it out of my sight! Now I know he'll get better because I can show God his necklace every time I pray, and God WILL hear me! Just watch, mommy! Just watch!"

"Thank you, doctor." said Tom and Maurene.

"Now you folks go home and try to get some rest. We WILL call if there is ANY change. You have my word!"

They all went home and tried to rest, but found it very difficult; given what had happened at the hospital. 'Code Blue' is a very serious thing. They'd almost lost Jerry. But at least now he was stable for the mean time. The only one who didn't seem to have any trouble resting was...Heidi. She slept as if she didn't have a care in the world- clenching Jerry's necklace tightly to her chest and repeating- "Thank you, Jesus!" over and over again.

Chapter 28
THE WAIT IS OVER

The next morning everyone, (especially Heidi), was anxious to get back to the hospital! She didn't know why- but she was sure that this was going to be a day for miracles!! She was SO excited!!!----This was Easter- but that didn't even cross any of their minds. They were only concerned about Jerry and what would happen today.

When they arrived at the CCU waiting room, Maurene and Heidi decided to go in first. (The truth of the matter was that Heidi started to the unit without even stopping at the waiting room; still clenching her dad's necklace). So Maurene followed her.

When they arrived at Jerry's room, the curtain was pulled half-way closed. Heidi started to cry, thinking the worst---but when Maurene peeked around the curtain; what she saw made her pass out! There were doctors and nurses around checking vital signs and instruments; but the most important thing was— Jerry was awake—(completely)!

After Maurene, came to she was in for another big surprise! When Maurene woke up; who was sitting there with her but Sandy!! Sandy sat there (wiping Maurene's face), while tears streamed down her face. "Can you ever forgive me"? She asked, as she hugged Heidi; who was also in tears.

"Sandy, is it really you? Are you really here, or am I dreaming/"

"I arrived in town last night around 11. How's Tom and Kirstin? How've you all been? I'm SO ashamed! I've been living alone for about two years now."

"Why didn't you come back, Aunt Sandy? We missed you so much!" cried Heidi, as she wrapped her arms around Sandy's neck and cried even harder.

"Yes, Sandy. Why didn't you at least write or call once in a while? It would have meant so much to all of us. You could have been dead for all we knew. Jerry blamed his problems with alcohol on losing you. What happened, Sandy?"

"I was foolish and stupid. When Bob and I left, I knew it hurt all of you—for which I'll always be sorry. I'll do ANYTHING to make up for the heartbreak I've caused; although I'll probably never be able to make up for it. I didn't call or write because I was so utterly ashamed of myself and didn't want to cause more pain. I hated myself for my stupidity and thought that everyone would be better off without me in their lives to mess 'em up further. I thought that if I forced myself out of the picture long enough that everyone would finally be able to heal and get on with their lives. I figured that I deserved to be lonely for the rest of my life after what I've done."

"What happened to you and Bob?"

"Well, we had been together for about eleven months when he started acting strange and distant. He was always a good provider; and that first eleven months was almost Heavenly. I thought. Then one day, right before Christmas, he sent me a dozen black roses with a Dear John letter attached. The note said that it was over; that he couldn't pretend any longer. It went on to say that he and his secret partner (of about ten year's duration) were going to live together and start an all-male adult club. I swear, Maurene, he had me completely fooled! This FLOORED me! I felt betrayed completely: exposed and violated beyond description! I couldn't face ANYONE! I've not even contacted my parents, because I didn't know what to say! When the Red Cross contacted me about Jerry, I left everything I had in Mississippi and boarded the first flight back I could catch. All I brought with me is what I had on my back. I didn't want anything else I had there. I felt so dirty every time I even looked at it! You know what I mean?"

"Oh, Sandy, that had to be awfully devastating! How'd you make it for two whole years believing that you had no one to turn to? I can't even imagine that feeling-and I thought I had it bad because of Jerry's alcoholism. At least I still had Heidi, Tom and Kirstin; how'd you ever survive?"

"Oh! Tom and Kirstin! How's my baby? I missed her so-o much, but didn't want to cause her any more pain. I thought if I stayed out of their lives long enough that they might be able to forget me, heal, and go on with their lives. After all, I didn't deserve them after what I'd done to them! How're they doing? Are they happy? I sure do hope they've been able to find the happiness that I wasn't good enough to give them. Please tell me that they did. I want them happy; I REALLY do!"

"Sandy, come with us for a moment. We have something to show you." And with that request, the three of them left the unit.

When they got back to the waiting room; they found Tom looking at a magazine, and Kirstin playing with her pocket game.

"Who's that lady with you, Aunt Maurene?" asked Kirstin.

Maurene gave her the 'sh!' sign just as Tom looked up from his reading. "Wha--?! Sandy, oh Sandy!" he shouted as he ran to embrace her with tears streaming down his face.

Mauren and Heidi went over to Kirstin; who was sitting there in shock. "Tom, why don't you and Sandy go downstairs and talk. Heidi and I will look after Kirstin.

"Thank you" they both said as they left the waiting room arm in arm.

"Was that my mommy?" asked Kirstin.

"Yes, honey-that IS your mother!" said Maurene as she took Kirstin in her arms

"Did she come back home to stay?"

"We sincerely hope so, Kirstin."

"I couldn't even remember what she looked like except for the wedding picture daddy cries over every night!"

Downstairs in the chapel, Tom and Sandy were discussing all the events that had brought her back. "Sandy, if you only knew what we've gone through- what I've gone through all this time!! I've never wanted anyone but you! And Kirstin—well—I've tried my best- but I don't know how good that was without a mother's influence around. She really needed you!"

"Oh, Tom! I'm so sorry I've hurt all of you-really I am."

"Why didn't you call or even send a card—at least for Christmas or her birthday?" She's grown up feeling like a freak. Feeling like everything was her fault—even though I've tried my best to reassure her that she had nothing to do with it. By not hearing from you she believed she was the reason you left—that she'd chased you away. It's really been tearing her apart—especially for the last year or so!"

"I know I've caused tremendous pain to everyone and I'm sorrier than I know how to express. The only thing I can say is I felt like I didn't deserve ANYONE after Bob left. I believed if I stayed out of everyone's life; that time would heal and help everyone forget me. I truly believed that I deserved to be alone for the rest of my life. I truly hate myself and really wouldn't blame any of you if you wanted nothing more to do with me. I honestly wouldn't! I didn't come back to try to hurt anyone anymore. I came back because of Jerry's condition. The Red Cross told me that you and Maurene had been trying to find me—that Jerry wasn't doing well. If you want me to I'll fade out of your life forever as soon as I find out Jerry's prognosis. I truly understand how you must hate me, I do!"

"That's NOT what I'm saying, Sandy. I've never wanted ANYONE but you; don't you understand? For the last three years it's just been Kirstin and me. Kirstin has filled my life with joy and encouragement in my darkest hours. And believe me; they're have been plenty of them! I've not been able to think about anyone but you and Kirstin!"

Chapter 29
HOME AT LAST

"Are you saying that it's okay for
me to come back home, Tom?"

"Yes, oh yes! That's what we've all
been praying for—that's All we've ever
wanted! Please? We need you, Sandy!"

"Oh, yes—but I really don't deserve it!
I'll spend the rest of my life working
to make it up to everyone! Thank
you, Tom—I really don't deserve your
love—but I'm thankful that I still
have it. Can you ever forgive me?"

"If you do come back; I'm
asking one thing of you."

"Anything, Tom, anything."

"Heidi and Kirstin started attending
'fun days' at this church down the
road from us with some friends or

theirs. They're really excited about it and wanted me to start going. I'm going to ask that you go with me on Sunday. Maybe they can help us with our issues, and help our marriage to become stronger. You game?"

"Anything if you'll take me back, Tom, anything! I never dreamed I could be getting my family back when the Red Cross contacted me. I knew I didn't deserve them---let alone everyone else! Thank you, Tom, thank you! I do so love you and Kirstin! I really do, honest! I'll do my best the rest of my life to prove it to you!! I will!"

Chapter 30
'THE SHOCK'

While Tom and Sandy were downstairs; Maurene had taken the girls in to see Jerry; who was still awake.

"He still might not be able to talk to you- but he IS awake now." They were told.

As they approached Jerry's room, Heidi couldn't control herself. "Daddy, oh daddy," she shouted as she ran to her dad's side, threw herself onto her dad's bed, and cried uncontrollably. "I'm so glad you're better. We've been so scared—but-I knew Jesus was going to help. I just knew He would! After all, He sent Aunt Sandy home, and now you're awake! Jesus really does love us, doesn't He?"

All of a sudden, Jerry's eyes started moving rapidly, and the instruments started recording problems.

"Mrs. Lipscomb, maybe you should take the girls out for a little while. We're afraid this has been too much excitement for him. We'll get him settled down, and you'll be able to come back in, okay?"

As they left the unit, Heidi couldn't stop crying: "Mommy, I'm really sorry. I didn't mean to hurt daddy—really, I didn't. I hope he's not gonna get worse again. This is all my fault. 'Jesus, please forgive me'. Mommy, can you and daddy forgive me? I'll be quiet from now on if Jesus helps him. I promise I will!!"

"Sweetheart, that's okay. I just believe daddy was so happy to see us, find out that we still loved him, and that Aunt Sandy was back. That's all. I believe he'll be okay. We'll just have to try not to excite him too much until he's a lot better, okay? You help me and I'll help you. But let's continue to ask Jesus to help us, okay?"

"Sure, mommy---and He will, too. Won't He?"

"Yes, sweetheart, I believe He will." Said Maurene as they approached the waiting room.

After they sat down; Tom and Sandy arrived back holding hands and looking quite intensely at each other. "We have an announcement for everyone; but we want to tell Jerry first! We'll be back out to tell all of you what we've decided, okay?" Tom and Sandy announced and headed for the unit.

"I'm sorry, guys, you can't go in there right now---we just came from him. He got overly excited and took a setback. They're working to stabilize him right now. Sorry." Maurene said with tears running down her cheeks.

"What happened to excite him so much that it hurt him?"

"It's all my fault." Said Heidi through veils of tears. "I didn't mean to—I just told him that we all loved him and wanted him back home---and that you came home again, Aunt Sandy! After I said that; his eyes started moving funny, the machines started making funny sounds, and they asked us to leave. I hope I didn't kill him, Aunt Sandy. I'll NEVER forgive myself if he doesn't come back to us. I KNOW I won't!" And with that; she broke down and wept more bitterly than before.

Chapter 31
THE REUNION

"Why don't you all take Heidi home for a while and see if you can console her? I'll stay here with Jerry, and call you the minute I learn something, I promise." Said Sandy. "And Heidi, it's okay. I know you didn't mean any harm to your dad. It's okay, honey. I'll talk to your daddy. He'll be okay. After all, like you told me---Jesus is helping him, and Jesus doesn't stop in the middle of a problem. You calm down now and let Jesus work, okay?"

"Well, if you're sure, Sandy. Thank you, I really don't think it'll do Heidi any good to stay here any longer today like this. Thanks."

"Tom; you and Kirstin go ahead and help Maurene. I'll call you. And thank you for your love and

for letting me come home. I'll
make it up to you, I promise."

"Are you sure, Sandy?" asked
Tom. "You gonna be alright?"

"I'll be fine now that I know I have
my family back. Go ahead—Kirstin
and Heidi need each other right now.
I'll see you later. I love you, Tom."

After Tom and Maurene left with the
girls, Sandy went back to the chapel.
"God, if you're really up there, and you
really DO care about your creation;
please hear my prayer. I know I don't
deserve or have any right to ask You
for anything; but I do have a few things
I'd like to talk with you about. First of
all---I've been sinfully stupid. I really
hate myself and am (from the bottom
of my heart) sorry for what I've done to
my family. I've broken the hearts deeply
of everyone I love---and almost killed
my brother. (The only family I have left).
I want to ask you to forgive me for my
stupid, sinful ways. Help me to make up
for all the pain I've inflicted upon all of

them, and get our lives back to where they were before---only more joyful and stable. I ask you to save my brother's life, and help him to give up his sinful ways; so he and his family can be happy together again. And ... (was interrupted by an announcement over the hospital intercom) "Will the family of Jerry Lipscomb please return to the CCU?"

With that, she left the chapel and all but ran to the unit. "What's wrong? Please tell me—what happened?" She questioned the nurse at the station.

"Are you the only one here?" she asked.

"Yes. The others took Heidi home to settle her down. She was afraid that she'd killed her dad!"

"Come with me."

As they approached Jerry's room Sandy was very surprised at what she saw: Jerry was fully awake. They had him propped in an upright position. When he saw Sandy, tears started flooding his face. His lips started to quiver as he tried to speak: "Sandimoridy, Sandimoridy!"

"What is he saying, doctor?"

"We don't really know. He was repeating the same jibberish before the setback. No one seems to be able to figure it ou...."

Just then, Jerry lifted his arms toward Sandy and he started crying even more.

Sandy ran to her brother's bedside and threw her arms around his neck. "Yes, Jerry, I'm home. Please---can you ever forgive me for what I've done to you? I was so stupid. I didn't think of anyone but myself; and I've really paid for my stupidity---but not nearly enough. I'll spend the rest of my life trying to make it up to all of you." And with that- she, too, started crying.

All of a sudden, Jerry's face broke open into a big smile and he went limp.

"Don't worry, Mrs. Massey, he's tuckered out. He just went to sleep. He'll probably be out for a while. We gave him something to help him rest. Why don't you go on home and get some rest yourself? You've been here all day, and it won't do him any good if you get down now. We'll let his wife know of ANY changes, okay?"

Sandy called Tom to pick her up feeling lighter than air. "Can we go by KFC on the way home? I want to pick up dinner for all of us. I believe there's cause to celebrate! I'll tell you about it when we get to Maurene's, okay?"

When they arrived at Maurene's, they were surrounded by hugs before they could even get to the door—with Heidi leading the way.

"Here; let me take that inside for you," said Tom.

Sandy couldn't hardly believe her eyes at all the acceptance, forgiveness, and love she was experiencing. 'I

really don't deserve ANY of this-thank
You, Jesus! Thank YOU for answering
my prayer so quickly- even though I
messed up royally!' she thought to
herself, as they all walked in together.

"What's up, Sandy? Did Jerry
come back? Why did you leave
him? You should've called!"

"Calm down, please. The medical staff
sent me home. I have great news to
tell you. That's why I'm here. This day
has been phenomenal. Better than I
could've ever even hoped for! Let's
eat and then I'll explain. I'm famished!
Anyone here like fried chicken?"

Heidi and Kirstin were the first to
shoot their hands up in the air. "Can
we ask God to bless the food before we
start eating? Pastor Higgy says that we
should always thank Him for it and ask
Him to bless it before we eat, okay?"

"I think we'd better in light of
what's happened today, don't
you?" Sandy answered.

"Dear God, we thank YOU for this food—and especially for bringing my mommy back home. Help me get to know her as well as everyone else did before she left...." Said Kirstin. "Yes, Lord, and bless this food we're about to eat; and help us grow strong in body and spirit. Help my daddy get better so we can be a happy family again. In Jesus' name. Amen."

"That was beautiful, girls!" said Sandy, with tears on her face as she hugged both girls tightly in a big group hug.

After they ate, everyone went into the living room and sat down with their milk and coffee; as Maurene brought in some pie she'd bought at the store on her way home from the hospital.

"Now tell us," said Maurene, "just what you meant by 'great news'. What exactly happened up there? Don't keep us in the dark any longer, please!"

"Well, let's see; where should I start? I have so-o-o much to tell you!"

"How 'bout from the beginning?"

"Well, okay. Tom and I are back together again! He's decided to give us another chance! You know, Maurene --- as I told you earlier--- I'd never dreamed of getting another chance with my family. I knew I *didn't deserve it!*".
"Yes," said Tom. But I gave her a condition to that .Didn't I, Sandy?"

"Yes, we're going to start going to 'God's House' with Heidi and Kirstin. We really (I really) need help to resolve past and present issues. Maybe that pastor can help us!"

"You won't be sorry, Aunt Sandy!" said Heidi. "You will love him; and he WILL help! He prayed with us. His church has been praying for all of us and here you are—home with us!"

"That's all wonderful; but, didn't you say that you would call us as soon as you found something out about Jerry?" asked Maurene. "Yes; and that's the other news I have to tell you. Make sure we're all braced----it's really nothing short of a miracle, I believe!"

"Well, spill it," said Tom. "Don't keep us in limbo, Sandy!"

"Okay, okay---here goes. Get ready—I told you it was almost unbelievable! After everyone left; I went back to the chapel I couldn't get back in to see Jerry. Believe it or not---I was down there on my knees pleading for everyone (especially Jerry): when all of a sudden the hospital intercom came on right in the middle of my prayer asking anyone who was there with Jerry to report to GGU. Of course I braced myself for the worst and kept praying for the best. When I got there, they ushered me into Jerry's room. Guys; Jerry was fully awake! He was sitting up with pillows behind him to prop him! I know he recognized me because he looked right at me, started crying, and tried to talk—but the only thing that came out was jibberuish. No one could make anything out of it! Then he did the unexpected! He lifted his arms out towards me and cried even more! I couldn't do anything but run to him and hug him—which made me cry!! I tried to apologize to him but; just as quickly as his arms raised—he went limp. The doctors helped him lie back down and told me they'd given him something to help him rest; and that I should try to rest also. It all happened so fast that I didn't have time to place that call! Please forgive me!!"

"Mommy, daddy's gonna be okay! I told you that if anyone could make a change, it'd be Aunt Sandy!" (This happened on Memorial Day, 1990.) The two girls got up, held hands, and started dancing around singing 'Amazing Grace'- to the 'Pepsi theme music.

This was just the beginning. It would be quite a lengthy recovery for Jerry.

Jerry remained in and out of consciousness for a while; but the two families continued getting together to try to heal themselves and bond.

Chapter 32
FOREVER IN OUR HEARTS SOCIETY

At God's House it was another canvasing day---but not for Sunday school. A new group had emerged to help with life and loss of loved ones.

After prayer, everyone grouped themselves together, and began their work. Ronald, Rosie, and Jenny were given Herald Corner Place Station Road-West, where the Numbsenses' lived.

As they approached the first house, they noticed a man outside working on his car. "Hello, sir!" Ronald called out.

"Hello, may I help you?" Carl asked.

"Well, actually my wife and I would like to talk to you and your wife for a moment- if we may. We promise not to be too long."

"I guess that would be okay. Let me get my wife." And he went inside to wash his hands.

"Honey, there's a couple outside who said they'd like to talk to both of us for a minute. Should I let them in? They have the prettiest little girl with them. I'm guessing about 2-3 years old."

"Sure, honey. I'll get some iced tea for them. Let them in; it'll be kinda nice to start visiting with someone again."

"Please pardon the wait; I had to wash my hands first. Come on in- my wife will join us in a minute. This is our son, Quentin."

"What a nice looking young man! What grade are you in, Quentin?"

"Uh, second, I think—right, dad?"

"Yes, we home school him."

"That's wonderful! We hope to home school our little Jennifer here in a couple of years. How is he doing with the home schooling?"

"He's doing great!"

At this point in the conversation, Betty walked into the room carrying a serving tray filled with glasses of iced tea, juice and cookies.

"Would you folks care for some tea and cookies? I brought juice for the children."

"Oh, thank you—you didn't have to go to all that trouble. We just wanted to talk to you for a moment about something very important. You see, about 10 years ago; (after we'd been married for about 2 years), we became pregnant and were so-o happy that nothing could get us down---or so we thought. We added a nursery to our home and had it fully furnished (although we didn't know the baby's gender). Then one day, into her sixth month, my wife called me home from work stating that something HAD to be wrong." Said Ronald. "When I got home, she was in such excruciating pain and hemorrhaging. I rushed her to the hospital immediately and called the doctor who met us there. It was already too late- the baby was gone and Rosie almost lost her mind. We wanted that baby so-o much!"

"Yes," said Rosie. "I was so-o devastated that I didn't care if I lived or died. I felt so guilty and useless! Girls have babies everyday (even out of marriage), and I couldn't even give life to one child who'd have two loving parents! What good was I? I didn't feel that I deserved to live!"

Ronald continued: "Then one day, a neighbor told us about this group------ "FOREVER IN OUR HEARTS". He said that he felt they might be able to help us. He also said that if we'd be willing to try it out, he'd take us there. We figured that we didn't have anything to lose- (after all we'd already lost everything- we thought); so we went with him. It has brought the salvation of our marriage!"

"Yes, and my sanity!" added Rosie.

"Anyway, we'd tried for several years to get pregnant again without any results come to find out; it seems that Rosie was unconsciously rejecting conception because of her fear of losing it again."

"Yes. 'FOREVER IN OUR HEARTS' is one of the (probably THE) most helpful groups we've ever been priviledged to know about. Would you folks happen to know someone who might be able to use help from people who've been through a situation like the one we've told you about?"

Carl's and Betty's eyes became wide with astonishment. "How did they know about us? Who sent them?" They thought.

"Who sent you?" They asked.

"No one, really---and yet someone." They answered.

"You see—'FOREVER IN OUR HEARTS' is a relatively new group from 'GOD'S HOUSE' down the road that's been formed to bring anyone dealing with loss together for group discussion, helps, friendship, bonding, and support. Losing someone you love is difficult. No matter how close or distant a family is----everyone needs some kind of help to get through it and go on with life. We've elected to go to visit 8 to 10 families a night to get the word out about this group and how much it's helped us cope and triumph over our loss. We believe that everyone---one time or other ---has had to deal with loss. If we can help someone cope--- and understand such---then we've also helped ourselves grow stronger in the process. Anyway, here's a leaflet describing the group and giving the address and times of the meetings. Would you be interested in going with us on Thursday evening to check it out; so you'll know first-hand what to tell others about 'FOREVER IN OUR HEARTS'?"

"This is very uncanny." Said Betty.
"You've almost described my
life until Quentin. This is weird!
Yes, I believe we would like to try
it out. Is there child care?"

"Don't worry about the children. They
have activity people providing games,
crafts, and refreshments. Jennifer
loves it! Here's our phone number.
Please call us if you need a ride, okay?"

"Okay, thank you. We certainly will
give this some thought, we promise."

"God bless you. Thanks for
the refreshments."

"You're welcome; and thank you."

Chapter 33
LONELY HEARTS, GOOD FRIENDS

After Rosie, Ronald, and Jennifer left; Betty and Carl sat down to talk. "What was THAT all about? That was so strange it was almost freaky!" Carl said.

"I know- it was almost like someone had been talking to them, perfect strangers, all about me." Said Betty. "I almost feel like we HAVE to go and check this out because of the sheer strangeness of it!" "Yeah; me, too." Said Carl.

On Thursday morning, Betty called Rosie about the group meeting. "Did you say that they meet at 6pm tonight?"

"Yes, did you decide to go?"

"Yes, we'll be going but we'll take our car. Carl doesn't get home until about 4:30 and we'll need to stop somewhere and grab something quick to eat on the way."

"Well, why don't you folks meet us at Mike's Burger Barn? I'm meeting Ronald there about 5. We'll wait to order till you get there. We can talk a little more and get to know each other a little better before we go to group. Okay?"

"Okay, that sounds fine. Quentin likes Mike's burgers. We'll probably see you about 5:15. Is that okay?"

"Fine; see you then. Bye!"

As Carl, Betty, and Quentin pulled into the parking lot at Mike's Burger Barn; they were surprised to see the Renners waiting outside the Building. "Been waiting long?"

"No. Actually we just arrived a few minutes ago. We thought

it'd be nice for all of us to go in together---that way no one would have to look around for seating."

"Oh, thank you."

"After they all sat down and gave their orders to the waiter; the children asked if they could play until the food arrived.

"Okay, for a little while--- but, be watching for the waiter to bring the food, okay?"

Quentin replied: "I'll keep an eye on Jennifer for you: if you want me to. I won't let her get hurt, okay? And I will watch for the food cause I'm hungry today, I promise!"

While the children played, the two couples took time to do a little comparing of their stories.

"The doctor told me at the time that I was too small—I'd never be able to carry the child full term— let alone deliver it!" said Rosie. "I

thought I was doomed to be barren
all my life. I didn't feel I was of use
to anyone if I couldn't even give
my husband ONE child to love."

"That's right." Ronald broke in. "She
even said that we needed a divorce
so that I could find someone worthy
of my love who could really fulfill
me and complete the union. But
I told her 'NO', that I married her
because I loved her—with or without
children—that we'd be okay!"

I was in really deep depression until
our neighbor convinced us to try
out "FOREVER IN OUR HEARTS"

"Well, what happened with us,"
started Betty; "was I was pregnant
and started hemorrhaging almost
right away. The pain was almost
deadly. So, I called Carl home to get
to the hospital. When we arrived,
I was ushered immediately to Dr.
Froyd's office where after examining
me thoroughly; he determined that
the baby was dead (inside my tubes).

He said that, given another 24 hours, I would have bled to death.

They treated me to blood builders; (I had already lost a copious amount of blood), and they feared for my life if I'd stayed home. Well, after that, I was afraid to get pregnant again; but, two years later, I had Quentin. I've been afraid to let him out of my sight----afraid if I did, somehow I'd end up losing him, too. That's why we've home schooled him, mainly. I mean it IS a better education than the public schools offer---but this way I know what he's being taught, and I know he's safe." Said Betty, with Carl echoing her words.

Just then the waiter arrived with their orders. Carl got up and ushered the children back to the table.

Chapter 34
THE TIE THAT BINDS

Upon arriving at the group meeting, Carl and Betty were astonished at the massive warm feeling of togetherness they felt almost immediately.

Pastor Higgenbotham, together with several others from the church membership led the whole group (about 150 total), in the singing of 'Blessed Be The Tie That Binds'--- then they prayed together (encircling the attendees)- that God's wisdom would prevail; and broke up into about 10 different groups with a qualified grief counselor heading each group.

Inside each group, the counselor had everyone join hands and hearts with each other, and unite in sincere prayer that God would guide each and every one to let go of the pain and release it to the spirit of prayer.

They were encouraged NOT to pray for themselves, but to pray for the person across the circle from them.

After the prayer was finished, they sat in desks around the room; were handed paper and pencils, and instructed to write their grief stories on the paper. Then, one by one, (starting with the counselor), each read his own story to the group; crumpled it into a ball, and placed it in a small waste basket in the center of the circle. Then they were given another sheet of paper and told that (at the end of the session) they were to write down their own plan for closure. Each couple was assigned 'Grief Buddies'- who were to check on each other twice a week to encourage each other to just let go and let God! The whole meeting took about 45 minutes to an hour At the end of the session they were dismissed to the large meeting room. Pastor Higgenbotham then prayed again for the group, asked if anyone needed special prayer, and dismissed the group.

Each counselor led his/her group out to the barn pit behind the church; carrying the waste basket from their group. Each basket was emptied into the pit ---lit on fire by Pastor Higgy---as the whole group was led in one more chorus of 'Blessed Be The Tie That Binds'. Then all went home.

Upon arriving at home Garl, Betty, and Quentin entered with new hope.

"Mommy, daddy that was fun. Can we go again? I made two new friends—not counting Jennifer because she's a girl. Can we?"

"Yes, Quentin, I believe we will. We've made some really nice friends, too. That was certainly different. I believe we'll be alright now, FINALLY!"

From that time on, you never saw a happier family than the Numbsenses; who were hardly ever seen by themselves again.

Chapter 35
A NEW BEGINNING

Tom and Sandy made good their promise to the girls and started attending services at God's House— but they didn't go alone; Maurene went with them. They all entered Christian counseling and found answers they had long been seeking.

It was now June 7, 1990; and Jerry had been in and out of consciousness for about 2-2 ½ months. The two families stayed faithful to visit Jerry often— making sure he knew that they loved him and had prayers going up for him.

On one such visit; as they approached the GGU unit, they were met by nursing staff. "We just moved him to a semi-private room on the 3rd floor. He woke up and started rallying. Sorry we didn't get to call you folks first; but

we had another emergency and needed
his room. He's in room 3641, bed 2.

They rushed down to Jerry's new
room to find another surprise:
Jerry was sitting up in a chair,
and he looked---good!!

In the days that followed, Jerry
continued to improve. They talked
to him every day---and he was able to
talk back to them---letting them know
that the only thing he remembered
about GGU was constantly thinking
about Sandy, Maurene, and Heidi.

"So that's what you were trying to
say! We couldn't figure out what
'sandimoridy' was, Jerry!"

"Sadimore, what?"

"You kept repeating our names
together over and over again,
but we couldn't understand
what you were trying to say!"

On June 14, 1990 Jerry was released from the hospital, and he never touched another drop of alcohol. He still had a difficult road to complete recovery, But, he had his whole family back---and they had their old Jerry back again. He didn't commit to God, but he didn't keep his family from attending. God would continue to deal with him for the rest of his life.

WHAT AN ADVENTURE!!!

BETRAYAL

SANDY LONGS FOR EXCITEMENT AND PURSUES IT WITH TOM'S BEST FRIEND; WITHOUT ANY FORETHOUGHT ON HER FAMILY'S BEHALF!

FEAR

BETTY LIVING IN FEAR OF LOSING HER SON; AND QUENTIN LIVING IN FEAR OF NEVER BEING ALLOWED TO BE NORMAL!

HOPELESSNESS

HEIDI AND MAURENE LIVING HOPELESS LIVES CAUSED BY BETRAYAL AND ADDICTION!

LOSS

ALL FAMILIES SUFFER SOME KIND OF LOSS---BUT AS KORAH AND LEVI DEMONSTRATE---HAPPINESS CAN BE RECOVERED IN SPITE OF LOSS!!!

Printed in the United States
By Bookmasters